Is Kisho the Class Dummy?

"You mean this is your second time in the second grade?" Elizabeth couldn't help asking.

Kisho nodded.

Lila looked suspicious. "How old are you going to be on your birthday?" she wanted to know.

"Nine," Kisho said. Everyone else in the second grade was seven or eight.

"Kisho must be dumb," Lila whispered to Jessica. "And I'm not going to be friends with a dumbo!"

Bantam Skylark Books in the SWEET VALLEY KIDS series

SWEET VALLEY KIDS
LEFT BACK!

Written by
Molly Mia Stewart

Created by
FRANCINE PASCAL

Illustrated by
Ying-Hwa Hu

A BANTAM SKYLARK BOOK ®
NEW YORK • TORONTO • LONDON • SYDNEY • AUCKLAND

RL 2, 005–008

LEFT BACK!
A Bantam Skylark Book / September 1992

*Sweet Valley High® and Sweet Valley Kids are
trademarks of Francine Pascal*

Conceived by Francine Pascal

*Produced by Daniel Weiss Associates, Inc.
33 West 17th Street
New York, NY 10011*

*Cover art by Susan Tang
Skylark Books is a registered trademark of Bantam Books, a
division of Bantam Doubleday Dell Publishing Group, Inc.
Registered in U.S. Patent and Trademark Office and elsewhere.*

ISBN 0-553-48005-7

Published simultaneously in the United States and Canada

*Bantam Books are published by Bantam Books, a division of Bantam Dou-
bleday Dell Publishing Group, Inc. Its trademark, consisting of the words
"Bantam Books" and the portrayal of a rooster, is Registered in U.S. Patent
and Trademark Office and in other countries. Marca Registrada. Bantam
Books, 666 Fifth Avenue, New York, New York 10103.*

PRINTED IN THE UNITED STATES OF AMERICA

CWO   0 9 8 7 6 5 4 3 2 1

To Kelly Rebecca Dyson

CHAPTER 1

The New Boy

"Ask her," Jessica Wakefield whispered to her twin sister, Elizabeth.

Elizabeth nodded, looking excited. She raised her hand.

"Yes, Elizabeth?" said Mrs. Otis, the twins' second-grade teacher.

Elizabeth cleared her throat. "We were just wondering when the new boy is getting here," she said.

Ever since Mrs. Otis had announced that a new student would be joining the class, Elizabeth and Jessica and their classmates had been looking forward to meeting him. Mrs.

Otis had told them that the new student, whose name was Kisho, would be coming on Friday. Today was Friday, and so far there had been no sign of Kisho.

Mrs. Otis smiled. "Kisho and his mother are in the principal's office right now," she said. "Mrs. Armstrong promised to bring Kisho down as soon as she could. I'm sure we won't have long to wait." The teacher walked over to her desk and picked up a book. "Now, while we're all waiting to meet Kisho, let's get started on our reading lesson for today," she said.

Elizabeth eagerly took out her reading book. She didn't really mind waiting, especially during reading. Reading was one of Elizabeth's favorite subjects. She loved books, and she often made up stories of her own about pirates or Indians. She was also good at sports, especially soccer, and she loved to play outside.

Jessica took out her reading book, too, but she wasn't as happy about it as her sister was. Jessica wanted to meet the new boy, and unlike Elizabeth she hated to wait. She was different from Elizabeth in other ways, too. Jessica liked reading sometimes, but her favorite thing about school was seeing her friends. She usually preferred to play inside with her dolls and stuffed animals rather than play outside and get her clothes dirty.

People often were surprised that Elizabeth and Jessica had such different interests, because the twins looked exactly alike. They both had blue-green eyes and long blond hair with bangs. Sometimes the twins liked to dress alike to confuse people. They always had a lot of fun watching their friends try to tell them apart. In fact, the twins always had a lot of fun together no matter what they did. Even though they enjoyed different things, Elizabeth and Jessica were best friends.

A few minutes later, Amy Sutton was taking her turn reading out loud when the principal, Mrs. Armstrong, walked into the classroom. The new boy was right behind her. He had straight black hair, olive skin, and black eyes. He was a little taller than the other second-grade boys.

"Good morning, everyone," Mrs. Armstrong greeted the class. She turned to Kisho and rested her hand on his head. "Mrs. Otis, this is Kisho Murasaki. Kisho, this is Mrs. Otis, your new teacher."

"Welcome to Sweet Valley Elementary School," Mrs. Otis said. "We've been looking forward to meeting you."

Kisho grinned. "Thanks."

"Have a good first day," Mrs. Armstrong told Kisho. She waved to the class and left the room.

Mrs. Otis gave Kisho a seat in the front row. "Why don't you tell us something about yourself, Kisho?" she suggested after he sat down.

"I just moved to Sweet Valley from Oklahoma," Kisho said. "I don't have any brothers or sisters. I like sports."

"I wonder if Kisho plays soccer," Todd Wilkins whispered to Elizabeth. Todd and Elizabeth played on the Sweet Valley Soccer League together.

"Let's ask him at recess," Elizabeth whispered back.

Mrs. Otis had each student say his or her name for Kisho. Then the teacher gave Kisho a copy of the reading book and helped him find the right page. "Let's finish our reading lesson," she said. "Charlie, I think it was your turn."

"'Mr. Brown had a big garden. He grew vegetables in the garden,'" Charlie Cashman read. "'His favorites were potatoes, carrots, and peas.'"

"Thank you, Charlie," Mrs. Otis said. "Lois, please continue."

"'Mrs. Brown liked vegetables, too,'" Lois Waller read. "'But she liked fruit even better. Mrs. Brown had three fruit trees. One grew apples, one grew oranges, and one grew cherries.'"

Mrs. Otis smiled. "Very good, Lois," she said. "Why don't you take over, Kisho?"

Kisho looked at the page. He took a deep breath.

"What's the first word, Kisho?" Mrs. Otis asked.

Kisho said the word to himself silently.

"To-get-her," Mrs. Otis sounded out. "To-gether."

"'Together,'" Kisho read slowly, "'Mr. Brown and Mrs. Brown made a . . .'" Kisho stopped reading and frowned. "What's the next word?" he asked.

"De-li-cious," Mrs. Otis said. "Delicious."

"'Together,'" Kisho read again, "'Mr. Brown and Mrs. Brown made a delicious dinner.'"

"Good job," Mrs. Otis said. "Jessica, please finish the paragraph."

Kisho looked happy that his turn was over. Elizabeth could tell that reading wasn't his favorite subject.

CHAPTER 2

Grandparents' Day Cards

"It's time for art," Mrs. Otis announced that afternoon. "Who's in charge of supplies this week?"

"I am!" Caroline Pearce yelled. "And so is Charlie." Caroline ran toward the art closet in the back of the room. Charlie followed her.

"Please get out the construction paper, paint, and crayons," Mrs. Otis told them. "It's almost Grandparents' Day," she said to the class. "We're going to work on cards to give to your grandmothers and grandfathers."

Winston Egbert showed Kisho where the students kept their smocks. Then they sat down in the seats Jessica and Elizabeth had saved for them at their art table. Amy Sutton, Todd, Lila Fowler, and Ken Matthews were sitting there, too.

"I'm going to draw my grandma and me riding bicycles," Amy announced. "My grandma loves to bike everywhere."

"Do you have a bicycle?" Elizabeth asked Kisho.

Kisho nodded. "Yes. It's green."

"How come you have such a funny name, Kisho?" Caroline asked, sitting down at the table.

Kisho was looking through a big box of crayons. "It's a Japanese name. Lots of people in Japan are named Kisho."

Amy frowned at her card. "I can't get the bicycle right," she complained.

"I'll help you if you want," Kisho said.

Amy leaned over to look at Kisho's card. "Wow! That's funny."

Jessica looked, too. Kisho had drawn himself—except that in the picture, Kisho's hair was blue.

"I couldn't find a black crayon," Kisho explained.

"You're a good artist," Jessica said.

"You sure are," Amy agreed. She pushed her card toward Kisho. "If you do the bicycle, I'll draw my grandma." Amy grinned. "I don't want her to have blue hair."

"My great-grandmother really does have blue hair," Winston said. "It's very light blue. She dyes it that color."

Jessica laughed. She had seen women with blue hair and thought they looked very strange. "Is she really old?" she asked Winston.

"She's eighty-five," Winston replied. "Her birthday was last week."

"My birthday is in eight days," Kisho said.

"Are you going to have a party?" Todd asked.

"Yes," Kisho said with a grin. "I get to invite the whole class. But since we just moved, my mom wants to have the party at the park. We can cook hamburgers on the grills there and play baseball."

"The park's not big enough for baseball," Lila said in her know-it-all voice. "You should have your party at Secca Lake. It has lots of grills and a big baseball field."

"Good idea," Kisho told Lila. "I'll tell my mom. I love baseball."

"Hey, Kisho," Todd said. "Do you play soccer?"

"You'd be good," Ken put in. "You're one of the biggest boys in the second grade."

"I'll bet you're even taller than Charlie," Winston added.

Kisho looked at the boys around the tables. "You guys will catch up to me," he said quietly. Then he went back to his drawing.

"I guess Kisho doesn't like soccer," Elizabeth whispered to Jessica.

Jessica shrugged. She didn't care whether Kisho liked soccer or not. The important thing was that Kisho was having a birthday party. Jessica loved parties. She could hardly wait.

CHAPTER 3

Party Invitations

"Hi, Jessica," Kisho said. It was Monday morning before school.

"Wrong twin," Elizabeth answered.

"At least I didn't call you Winston," Kisho said, smiling.

Elizabeth laughed. "It must be hard learning so many new names."

"It's not too bad," Kisho told her. "Everyone is helping me."

Jessica skipped up to them. "Are you talking about the party?"

"Party?" Kisho asked. "What party?"

"Your birthday party," Jessica reminded him. "Did you forget?"

"Of course not. I'm just joking," Kisho said, pulling two envelopes out of his spelling book. "Here are your invitations. The party's on Saturday."

"Thanks," Elizabeth said.

"We'll be there for sure," Jessica added.

"I've got to hand out the rest of these before the bell rings," Kisho told them. "See you later." He ran off.

"Hi," Amy said, as she and Eva Simpson came over.

Eva waved her invitation in the air. "Did you get yours?"

"Yes," Elizabeth and Jessica answered at the same time.

"I can't wait," Amy said. "I bet the party will be a lot of fun."

Jessica read her invitation again. "Maybe we can take pedal boats out onto the lake," she said, getting more excited with every word.

The bell rang, and everyone sat down. Soon it was time for math. "Today we'll go over the multiplication tables for times two and times three," Mrs. Otis announced.

"Yuck," Jessica whispered to Elizabeth.

Elizabeth smiled. She knew that Jessica didn't like to multiply. Elizabeth was usually very good at math, but even she had to admit that multiplication was hard.

Mrs. Otis wrote ten problems on the board. "Bring your work up to me when you finish," she said.

Elizabeth was only on the third problem when Kisho went up to Mrs. Otis. "One hundred percent correct," Elizabeth heard Mrs. Otis say. Elizabeth was very surprised.

16

Getting all the right answers on multiplication problems was amazing.

Mrs. Otis wrote down some more problems for Kisho. "Try these," she said. "It looks like you're ready to multiply by three."

"OK," Kisho said. He sat back down.

Jessica leaned forward in her seat. "How come you're so good at multiplication?" she asked Kisho.

"I studied it in Oklahoma," Kisho explained.

"You learned multiplication in the first grade?" Caroline asked. Her seat was next to Kisho's.

"No," Kisho said slowly. "In the second."

"You learned them at the beginning of this year?" Jessica asked. She looked confused.

Kisho shook his head. "No, I was in the second grade last year."

"You mean this is your second time in the second grade?" Elizabeth couldn't help asking.

Kisho nodded.

Lila looked suspicious. "How old are you going to be on your birthday?" she wanted to know.

"Nine," Kisho said. Everyone else in the second grade was seven or eight.

"Kisho must be dumb," Lila whispered to Jessica.

"He can't be dumb. He already knows how to multiply," Jessica pointed out.

Lila shook her head. "Kisho knows how to multiply because he's a year older than us. He's *supposed* to know stuff we don't know. But the teachers wouldn't let him go on to third grade, so he must be dumb."

Jessica thought for a moment. "You're right, I guess."

"I'm not going to be friends with a dumbo," Lila said.

"Me, neither," Jessica agreed.

"And I'm not going to his party," Lila added. "Even if it is at Secca Lake."

"We're not going, either," Jessica said.

Elizabeth was listening. She looked worried. "But Jessica," she protested. "You already told Kisho we'd go."

"I changed my mind," Jessica said.

Elizabeth didn't know what to think. She just hoped Kisho hadn't overheard them calling him a dumbo.

CHAPTER 4

Dumbo

As soon as the bell for recess rang, Jessica was out of her seat. "I want to go on the swings," she said, grabbing Elizabeth's hand. "Come on!"

Jessica and Elizabeth ran out to the playground and headed toward the swing set. Amy and Eva were already there. The twins picked swings next to each other.

"What are you going to get Kisho for his birthday?" Amy asked Elizabeth.

"I don't know," Elizabeth answered. "I guess we'll buy him something at the mall."

"We're not going to Kisho's party," Jessica spoke up.

Amy was surprised. "Why not?"

"This is Kisho's second time in the second grade," Jessica told her friends. "He's a repeater."

"So?" Amy said with a shrug.

"What are you guys talking about?" Lila asked, as she and Ellen Riteman finished playing hopscotch and ran to the swing set.

"The dumbo," Jessica said.

Ellen and Lila laughed.

"I don't get it," Elizabeth said. "On Friday, you all liked Kisho."

"That was different," Lila said, shaking her head. "On Friday, we didn't know he'd been left back."

"Shh!" Jessica interrupted. "Here he comes."

Kisho was racing against Winston, Todd,

and Charlie. He was in the lead. "I win this time," Kisho shouted when he reached the swings.

Jessica jumped up. "Let's go play jump rope," she said to the others. "I just got tired of swinging."

"Yeah," Lila said. "Let's go. We don't want to hang around with a dummy."

"Come on," Jessica said to Elizabeth. "Aren't you coming?"

Elizabeth got up slowly. "Well, OK."

"See you later," Amy said. "I'm staying here with Kisho."

Lila shrugged her shoulders as she started to walk away. Then she turned around. "Wait a second," she said to Kisho. "I can't come to your party."

"Neither can I," Ellen said. "We don't go to parties given by dummies."

Jessica, Lila, Ellen, and Todd laughed.

Elizabeth felt unhappy as she watched. She noticed that Amy, Winston, and Charlie looked as if they were unhappy, too. Elizabeth was a little surprised that Charlie wasn't teasing Kisho along with the others. Sometimes he could be a bully.

"I'm not coming to the party, either," Jessica said. "I have a feeling I wouldn't have any fun. I don't like to play with rattles or listen to nursery rhymes."

Kisho's face turned red. He jumped off the swing and ran to the far side of the playground.

Lila smiled. "I guess we can stay now," she said, sitting on one of the swings.

"Yeah," Jessica said. "Now it's safe."

Charlie stood up. His hands were clenched into fists. "You guys leave Kisho alone!" he yelled. "Stop teasing him—or else!" Then Charlie stomped away after Kisho.

CHAPTER 5

Kisho's Adventures

When the twins got to school the next morning, Elizabeth saw Charlie talking to Kisho at the back of the room. "I'm going to go talk to them," she said, pointing to the boys.

"OK," Jessica muttered. "But I don't know why you want to talk to a dumbo like Kisho."

Elizabeth didn't answer. She walked back to join the boys.

"Hello," Kisho said quietly.

"Hey, guess what, Elizabeth? Kisho just told me he was born in Japan," Charlie said.

"Really?" Elizabeth asked.

Kisho nodded. "We left Japan when I was four."

"Where did you move to?" Elizabeth asked.

"New York City," Kisho said.

"Wow," Charlie said. "What was it like?"

"Big!" Kisho replied.

Elizabeth and Charlie laughed.

"Then we moved to Oklahoma," Kisho explained. "And now Sweet Valley."

"Did you like moving so often?" Charlie asked.

"Not really," Kisho answered. "I didn't have a choice, though. My mom and dad are both professors—they teach in colleges—and they've had lots of different jobs. But they told me they think we'll stay in Sweet Valley for a while."

"I hope so," Elizabeth said. "Hey, Kisho, did you have to repeat the second grade because you were always moving?" Elizabeth hoped her question wouldn't make Kisho angry.

But Kisho didn't look angry at all. "I *have* missed lots of school," he said. "Also, I learned Japanese before I learned English. I don't have a problem speaking, but I still don't read English very well."

Elizabeth thought not being able to read would be horrible. She smiled at Kisho. "Mrs. Otis is a good teacher," she said. "You'll learn fast."

Kisho nodded. "I want to learn. I don't mind repeating the second grade. I just wish everyone would stop teasing me. In my old school, nobody acted like being left back was a big deal."

Elizabeth frowned. She wanted to make the other kids stop teasing Kisho, but she needed time to think of a plan. "Do you miss

Oklahoma?" she asked, trying to change the subject.

"A little," Kisho said. "But one of my grandfathers lives here in California. I like that because my other grandparents live in Japan. I hardly ever get to see them. Besides, we might go back to Oklahoma to visit—on an airplane."

"Cool," Charlie said. "I've never been on a plane."

"I went for the first time when my family took a trip to the Grand Canyon," Elizabeth said. "It was awesome."

"I've been on a plane three times," Kisho said. "When we moved from New York to Oklahoma, I even took photos out of the airplane window. Everything looked tiny."

"Cool!" Charlie said again.

"You guys should come over to my house

tomorrow," Kisho suggested. "I could show you the photographs."

"I'll ask my parents tonight," Elizabeth promised.

"Me, too," Charlie said. "And today after school, let's play space explorers at the park."

"OK," Kisho said. He gave them both a big smile. "We'll have a great time."

The bell rang and Kisho ran for his seat. Elizabeth started to head for hers, but Charlie grabbed her arm. "You're wondering why I'm being nice to Kisho, aren't you?" he asked.

"A little bit," Elizabeth admitted. She *had* been wondering about that. Usually Charlie never passed up a chance to make fun of someone.

"Well, I can be nice to anyone I want," Charlie said.

Elizabeth nodded. Charlie was right. He

was allowed to be nice, no questions asked. *I'm allowed to be nice, too,* Elizabeth reminded herself. *No matter what Jessica thinks.*

CHAPTER 6

Dumbo's Friend

After school, Jessica and Elizabeth rode their bikes to the park.

"I promised Kisho and Charlie I'd play space explorers with them," Elizabeth told Jessica, as soon as they parked their bikes. "Do you want to play, too?"

"With those two dumbos?" Jessica shook her head. "No way!"

"Then I'll see you later," Elizabeth said, as she ran off toward the jungle gym.

Jessica felt grouchy. She didn't want Elizabeth to play with Kisho and Charlie. It embarrassed her. She looked around the park and saw Lila waving at her.

Lila let the jump rope she was holding fall to the ground. "Hi, Jessica!" she shouted. "Aren't you coming over?"

Jessica walked slowly. "Hi," she said to Lila, Ellen, and Caroline. "Have you been here long?"

"Just a little while," Caroline answered. "Where's Elizabeth?"

"She's playing with Kisho," Jessica answered quickly.

"I saw her talking to him this morning at school," Ellen said.

Lila laughed. "Maybe Elizabeth likes Kisho."

"No, she doesn't," Jessica said. "She just feels sorry for him."

"Really?" Lila said, grinning. "Well, *I* think Elizabeth likes him."

"Elizabeth likes *everyone*," Ellen pointed out. "But I guess now she even wants to be friends with dummies and bullies."

"She does not," Jessica yelled. "Just you watch!" Jessica marched over to where Elizabeth was playing.

"Be careful," Charlie shouted when Jessica came near. "I'm pointing my ray gun at you."

"Hi, Jessica," Kisho called out. "Do you want to play with us?"

Jessica didn't answer Kisho. "I have to talk to you, Elizabeth," she said. "It's important." Then she stomped away.

Elizabeth hurried after her. "What's wrong, Jess?"

"I want you to stop being that dumbo's friend," Jessica said, turning to face her sister.

"Kisho's not dumb," Elizabeth insisted.

36

"Then why was he left back?" Jessica demanded.

Elizabeth looked at the ground. "I don't know. But it doesn't matter. I like Kisho. I wish everyone would stop being mean to him."

"What about me? Lila and Ellen are teasing *me* now," Jessica said. "It's awful. They'll stop if you quit playing with Kisho."

Elizabeth didn't say anything for a minute. She wanted time to think. "Why don't we just go home," she said finally.

"All right," Jessica agreed. She knew she wasn't going to have any fun at the park today.

Elizabeth and Jessica got their bikes and rode home. Elizabeth was silent the whole way. Jessica hoped that meant Elizabeth was busy thinking about not being Kisho's friend anymore.

"Hi, girls," Mrs. Wakefield said, when they

got home and came into the kitchen. She was chopping cheese, lettuce, tomatoes, and onions for tacos. Mr. Wakefield was stirring a skillet of hamburger meat. "How was the park?"

"OK," Elizabeth muttered. "We didn't stay long."

"Is something wrong?" Mr. Wakefield asked.

"Not anymore," Jessica said, tasting some of the cheese her mother had just grated. "I love tacos."

"Well, they're almost ready," Mr. Wakefield said. "Why don't you two set the table?"

"Do we have to?" Jessica complained.

Elizabeth laughed. She knew how much Jessica hated to do chores. "The faster we set the table, the faster we get to eat," Elizabeth pointed out.

Jessica didn't need to be told twice. She arranged the plates and glasses as Elizabeth

38

put out spoons, forks, and knives. Steven, the twins' older brother, came into the kitchen and poured drinks for everyone in the family.

"Mom," Elizabeth said, after everyone sat down. "How come some kids have to repeat a grade?"

"Because they're stupid," Steven answered before Mrs. Wakefield could say a word.

"See, I told you," Jessica said, looking at Elizabeth.

Mrs. Wakefield shook her head. "That's not true. Everyone learns at a different pace. Some kids just need more time."

"And that doesn't mean they're not smart," Mr. Wakefield added.

Jessica took a big bite of her taco. She still thought Kisho needed extra time because he was dumb. What other explanation could there be?

39

CHAPTER 7

Secret Plans

The next afternoon, Elizabeth, Charlie, and Kisho waited in front of school for Mrs. Murasaki to pick them up and take them to Kisho's house to play.

From the sidewalk, Elizabeth could see Jessica in the school bus. Her sister was sitting next to the window, with a big frown on her face. Elizabeth knew Jessica was unhappy that she was going to Kisho's house.

"There's my mom," Kisho said.

A red car pulled up to the curb. "Hello, kids," Mrs. Murasaki called. "Climb in."

Elizabeth, Charlie, and Kisho got into the

car. "Mom, this is Elizabeth, and this is Charlie," Kisho said.

Mrs. Murasaki smiled. "I'm glad you could come over and play with Kisho today. Kisho loves to have friends over."

Elizabeth smiled, too. She thought Kisho's mother was nice.

When they got to Kisho's house, Mrs. Murasaki made Charlie, Elizabeth, and Kisho a snack. "Let's go see my room," Kisho suggested as soon as they had finished eating.

Kisho's room was a mess. There were boxes everywhere. Some were open, with clothes spilling out of them. Others were still taped shut. "My mom and dad are going to help me unpack this weekend," Kisho explained. He frowned. "But I'm kind of messy, anyway."

Elizabeth and Charlie laughed. "So am I," Charlie said. "Does that mean you don't know where the photos you took from the airplane are?"

Kisho looked around. "Well, I know they're here somewhere," he said.

"OK, let's start looking," Elizabeth suggested. She lifted the lid on a small box near the bed. "You've got nothing but videos here."

Charlie opened another box. "Sheets and curtains," he said. He stuck out his tongue. "Boring."

Elizabeth untaped a box near her feet. "Books." She started to look at the different titles. "*Sailor Seagull*. This one is good."

"I haven't read it yet," Kisho said. He looked sad. Elizabeth knew Kisho was thinking about how the kids at school teased him. It made her feel awful.

"Kisho, come quick," Mrs. Murasaki called.

Charlie, Elizabeth, and Kisho ran down

the stairs. Mrs. Murasaki was talking on the phone, but she was speaking in a different language. Elizabeth couldn't understand a single word she was saying. Kisho started jumping up and down.

Charlie and Elizabeth exchanged puzzled looks.

"Let me talk! Let me talk!" Kisho yelled.

Mrs. Murasaki handed Kisho the phone. He started to speak. Now Elizabeth couldn't understand what *Kisho* was saying.

"Kisho's grandmother is calling from Japan," Mrs. Murasaki explained. "She speaks only Japanese."

Elizabeth listened to Kisho. She tried to figure out what he was saying, but she couldn't understand one word.

"Wow!" Charlie whispered to Elizabeth. "Japanese is really different than English."

Elizabeth nodded. "It's neat," she whispered back.

"That was my grandma," Kisho said, after he gave the phone back to his mother. "She's coming to visit next month. I'm going to take her to a baseball game."

"I didn't know you could still speak Japanese," Charlie said.

"My parents and I speak Japanese a lot at home," Kisho said. "Come here, I want to show you something."

Kisho led the way back to his bedroom. He pulled a book out of the box Elizabeth had been looking in. "This book is written in Japanese," he said, handing it to Elizabeth.

Elizabeth opened the book as Charlie peered over her shoulder.

Kisho smiled. "You just opened to the end of the story," he said. "In Japan, books start in the back and finish in the front."

Elizabeth opened the book from the back. Inside, there were rows of lines that looked like drawings. Elizabeth couldn't tell if they were letters or words. "Can you read this?" she asked.

Kisho nodded. He took the book and read a few lines in Japanese. Then he switched back to English. "It means, once there was a boy who lived in an apartment with seventeen cats," he explained. "Japanese is printed from the top down, instead of left to right like English."

Elizabeth shook her head. No wonder it was hard for Kisho to read English. Japanese and English had almost nothing in common.

"My grandparents came to the United States from Italy," Charlie spoke up. "When they got here, they didn't speak any English at all. Lots of people made fun of them. Sometimes, people still tease my grandfather. He says some words a little funny."

"That's terrible," Elizabeth said. Now she thought she knew why Charlie was being nice to Kisho. Charlie understood what it was like to be teased for being different.

"Do you speak Italian?" Kisho asked Charlie.

"A little," Charlie said. "My mom and my grandparents taught me."

"Since we moved to Sweet Valley, my grandfather is helping me with my Japanese," Kisho said proudly. "I always want to be able to speak it."

"Wouldn't it be great if Mrs. Otis taught in Japanese one day?" Charlie said. "Everyone would be totally confused."

"And the next day, class could be in Italian," Kisho added.

Charlie smiled. "Lila and Ellen would stop laughing then."

Elizabeth's mouth dropped open. "Kisho," she said. "I know how to make the kids at school stop teasing you."

Kisho's eyes widened. "Tell me."

CHAPTER 8

Different People

"Here come Charlie and Kisho," Jessica said. "What do you think they want?"

It was Thursday morning. Jessica and Elizabeth were standing near their desks, waiting for the bell to ring.

Elizabeth shrugged. "Wait and see," she answered.

"Hi!" Kisho said, as he and Charlie walked up to the twins.

Charlie glared at Jessica. "We have to talk to Elizabeth—alone."

Jessica crossed her arms. "I'm not going

anywhere," she huffed. "You can't order me around."

"It's OK, Charlie," Elizabeth said. "Don't worry about Jessica. Did you talk to your mom?"

Charlie glared at Jessica again. Then he smiled at Elizabeth. "Yes. She thought it was a great idea."

"I talked to my mom, too," Kisho said. "She thought it was a *terrific* idea."

"What's a terrific idea?" Jessica wanted to know.

"It's a surprise," Elizabeth said, smiling.

"That's right," Kisho said. "All we have to do now is talk to Mrs. Otis."

"When?" Charlie asked, just as the bell rang.

"Let's do it at lunch," Kisho suggested. "That way no one else will be around." He gave Jessica a mysterious smile.

"OK," Charlie and Elizabeth agreed.

"Ask Mrs. Otis what?" Caroline asked. Jessica spun around. She hadn't heard Caroline come up behind them.

"None of your business, busybody," Charlie said with a frown.

"You'll find out soon enough," Elizabeth said.

Caroline liked to know everything that happened in Mrs. Otis's class. But this time she didn't seem to be too curious. "It doesn't matter. Nothing you have to ask can be very interesting," she said to Kisho. "After all, you *are* the class dummy."

"Good morning, Caroline. Good morning, Kisho," Mrs. Otis greeted them.

Caroline gasped. *She* hadn't heard Mrs. Otis come up behind *her*. Elizabeth, Kisho, Charlie, and even Jessica smiled.

"OK, take your seats, everyone," Mrs. Otis said.

Mrs. Otis took attendance. Then she walked around to the front of her desk. "The world is a big place," the teacher said. "There are many, many kinds of people living in it. These people speak different languages, eat different foods, do different kinds of work, and have different kinds of ideas."

Jessica leaned over to Elizabeth. "What is Mrs. Otis talking about?" she whispered. "I thought we were studying multiplication."

"Shh," Elizabeth said. "Listen."

"The United States is an interesting place. All sorts of people from all over the world have come here to live," Mrs. Otis continued. "When people first come to the United States, they have a lot to adjust to. They have to learn to communicate with their new neighbors. They have to get used to eating American food. It takes them a while to learn everything. But that doesn't mean they're stupid. If we're patient with them while they learn, we usually find out they have something to teach us, too—a new word, maybe, or a new recipe, or a new idea. And everyone should remember that there are differences between people born in the same country. Each of you like different things, and you all do better in certain classes than in others."

"I think Mrs. Otis is talking about Kisho," Jessica whispered again.

Elizabeth nodded. "She's telling Caroline to be nicer."

Jessica didn't answer. She knew Mrs. Otis didn't just want Caroline to be nicer. She wanted *all* of them to be nicer. Jessica was beginning to think that wouldn't be such a bad idea. If everyone was friends with Kisho again, then Lila and Ellen wouldn't tease her just because Elizabeth was nice to him.

"Most of you were born in the United States," Mrs. Otis went on. "But remember, not too long ago, someone in your family came here from far away. When they first got here, they needed someone to welcome them. Your relatives would want you to be nice to the people who are just arriving now."

Kisho and Charlie both turned around and smiled at Elizabeth. Elizabeth smiled back, and winked at them.

"Mrs. Otis is going to like our idea," she whispered to Jessica.

"Can you tell me what it is now?" Jessica asked.

"You'll find out tomorrow," Elizabeth said

firmly. "It'll be a surprise. You just have to wait one day."

"OK," Jessica said. She loved surprises—but she hated to wait.

CHAPTER 9

The Surprise

The next morning, Elizabeth and Jessica rushed to the bus stop. Elizabeth wanted to make sure they got to school on time.

"Please tell me what's going to happen," Jessica begged when they sat down on the bus.

"No way," Elizabeth said. "You'll have to wait like everybody else."

Jessica laughed. "I'm excited, and I don't even know why."

At school, as soon as everyone had settled into their seats, Mrs. Otis made an announcement. "Today, thanks to Elizabeth,

Kisho, and Charlie, we're going to have two special visitors," she said. "Kisho is meeting them in the office right now."

A few minutes later, Kisho walked into the classroom. An elderly man and woman were with him.

"Why don't you introduce our visitors, Kisho?" Mrs. Otis suggested.

"Sure," Kisho said. "This is my grandfather, Mr. Murasaki. And this is Mrs. Gangemi—"

"My grandmother," Charlie interrupted. "They're going to tell us about moving to America."

"This is the surprise," Elizabeth whispered to Jessica.

"I like it," Jessica said. "This is going to be *much* better than multiplication!"

Mrs. Gangemi went first. "I was born in southern Italy, in a town called Palermo. I came to America when I was eleven years old."

Mrs. Otis pulled down the world map from above the blackboard. Charlie came to the front and pointed out Italy and then Palermo.

"I still remember coming into the harbor of New York City on the boat," Mrs. Gangemi went on. "The buildings in America looked very tall and new. Not at all like Italy." She told them all about the adjustments she'd had to make in her new home, and how helpful and friendly her neighbors had been.

When Mrs. Gangemi was finished, Mr. Murasaki told the class he had been born in Aomori, Japan. He had lived there until just three years ago. Kisho pointed out Japan and Aomori on the map.

"For one so old it is hard to learn," Mr. Murasaki said. "Every day, I must study English many hours, just like you do at school. Kisho's English is now better than mine. Sometimes, he teaches me new words."

"We're even," Kisho called out. "Grandfather helps me with my Japanese."

Mrs. Otis smiled. "Could you write some Japanese on the board for us?" she asked Kisho.

Kisho picked up a piece of chalk and wrote his name in Japanese.

"Wow! Japanese is pretty," Caroline said.

Jessica nodded. "It looks so different."

"Does anyone have a question?" Mrs. Otis asked.

Lois Waller raised her hand. "Why don't we learn a word in Japanese and one in Italian?" she suggested.

"That's a good idea," the teacher agreed. "Why don't you come up to the board and write down a word you'd like to learn?"

Lois's cheeks turned pink. But she got up and wrote "good" on the board.

Mr. Murasaki wrote the Japanese word for good. He said it sounded like *yoi*. Then Mrs. Gangemi wrote *bene* on the board. That meant good in Italian.

"Does anyone know how to say good in another language?" Mrs. Otis asked.

Eva Simpson knew how to say good in French. It was *bon*. Ken knew how to say good in German. It was *gut*. Lila knew how to say good in Spanish. It was *bueno*. Counting English, Mrs. Otis's class knew how to say good in six different languages.

"People who came to the United States spoke all of these languages," Mrs. Otis told the class. "These—and many more."

It was time for Mrs. Gangemi and Mr. Murasaki to go. Mrs. Otis turned to the class. "Do you have anything to say?"

"Thank you!" everyone yelled at once.

"Happy Grandparents' Day," Kisho added.

When the bell for recess rang a few hours later, everyone ran out to the playground. Instead of playing games, most of Mrs. Otis's students practiced their new words.

"Mr. Murasaki was neat," Jessica said, as she climbed the jungle gym.

"I liked him, too," Elizabeth said.

Jessica sat down on the top bar. Elizabeth sat next to her. The twins could see all of their friends running around the playground.

"You know, I don't think Kisho is dumb anymore," Jessica admitted. "I can't speak Japanese—but that doesn't make me stupid. I guess Kisho just needs more time to learn to read."

Elizabeth grinned. "I think you're right."

Jessica started to climb back down. "I had an idea, too."

"What?" Elizabeth asked as she climbed down after her sister.

"Remember that box of sixty-four crayons we saw at the card store in the mall?" Jessica asked.

"Yes," Elizabeth said. "They were great."

"I think Kisho would like them, don't you?" Jessica said. "I think it would be a good birthday present."

Elizabeth smiled. "Does that mean you want to go to Kisho's party?"

"Sure," Jessica said. "Everyone's going."

Elizabeth jumped from the lowest bar and landed in the sand. "It sounds like the perfect present," she agreed.

CHAPTER 10

Happy Birthday

Jessica and Elizabeth were ready for Kisho's party. They were wearing matching denim shorts and their favorite T-shirts. Todd's mother, Mrs. Wilkins, was going to pick them up and drive them to Secca Lake for the party.

Elizabeth and Jessica were watching Mrs. Wakefield wrap the box of crayons that they had bought for Kisho.

"Mom," Jessica said. "Yesterday at school, we found out Kisho's family is from Japan. Charlie's grandmother is from Italy. Do you know where we're from?"

"Yes," Mrs. Wakefield said with a smile. "Your great-great-grandmother came to America from Sweden in 1866. Her name was Alice Larson and she was just sixteen years old when she moved to this country."

"Do you know how to say good in Swedish?" Elizabeth asked.

Mrs. Wakefield laughed. "That's one of the few Swedish words I do know. It's *god.*"

"Now we can say good in seven languages," Jessica said.

Just then they heard the beeping of a car horn.

"That must be Mrs. Wilkins," Mrs. Wakefield said. She handed Jessica the beautifully wrapped present. "Have a good time."

A short while later, the twins were at Secca Lake. Everyone from Mrs. Otis's class was at Kisho's birthday party. There was a table full of presents and a table full of food. But something important was missing.

"Where's the cake?" Elizabeth asked Kisho.

"We're going to have Japanese desserts," Kisho explained.

After everyone sang, "Happy Birthday," Kisho and his parents passed out to each person something that looked like a hamburger bun. "These are called *manju*," Kisho said.

Jessica bit into hers. It had dark red stuff inside. "What is this?" she asked Kisho.

Kisho laughed. "Tell me if you like it first."

"I do," Jessica said. "It's sweet."

"That red stuff is made from beans," Kisho said.

Jessica made a face, but then she smiled. "I like it anyway."

"Hey, Kisho," Todd called. "Why don't we play a Japanese game?"

"OK, let's play baseball," Kisho suggested.

"Baseball isn't a Japanese game," Elizabeth said.

Kisho laughed. "Baseball started in America. But everyone loves it in Japan, too. There are Japanese sports like judo, but I like baseball best."

"OK," Todd said. "I'll play second base."

"I'm not very good at baseball," Caroline said. "You have to be on my team, Kisho."

"No way!" Lila yelled. "Kisho is going to be on *my* team."

"Kisho has lots of friends now," Elizabeth said to Charlie. "I've hardly gotten a chance to talk to him today."

Charlie grinned. "I know. It's *bene*."

"Yes," Elizabeth agreed. "Really *yoi*."

"*Gut*," Charlie said. "Or *bon*."

"*Bueno*," Elizabeth said. "And very, very GOOD!"

* * *

"Kisho's party was really fun," Jessica told her mother.

Mrs. Wakefield was driving the twins, Todd, and Caroline home from Secca Lake.

"Did Kisho like his crayons?" Mrs. Wakefield asked.

"Yes," Elizabeth said. "He got a lot of other great presents, too."

"Did you see what Charlie gave him?" Todd asked.

Caroline stuck out her tongue. "An ugly astronaut's helmet."

"I thought it was neat," Elizabeth said.

"Me, too," Todd said. "Kisho told me he might be an astronaut for Halloween. It would be easy, since he already has the mask."

"He can even get rocks from the park and pretend they're moon rocks," Elizabeth said.

"*I* wouldn't want to be an astronaut for

Halloween," Jessica said. "I want to be something beautiful."

"Like what?" Caroline asked.

Jessica shook her head. "I don't know. I still have to think of something."

Mrs. Wakefield pulled up in front of the Wilkinses' house.

"You'd better think of something fast," Todd told Jessica as he jumped out of the car. "Halloween is almost here."

"Bye, Todd," Elizabeth, Jessica, and Caroline yelled.

Todd ran up to his house and let himself in the door.

Jessica bounced up and down in her seat as Mrs. Wakefield started toward the Pearces'. "I can't wait for Halloween to get here."

"Me, neither," Elizabeth and Caroline agreed.

"I want to win the Best Costume award at school," Elizabeth added as Mrs. Wakefield pulled up in front of Caroline's house.

Caroline opened the car door and climbed out. "There's no way you're going to win the Best Costume award," she said, turning to face Elizabeth.

"How come?" Elizabeth asked.

"Because *I'm* going to win it!" Caroline told her.

Will Caroline win the class award for best Halloween costume? Find out in Sweet Valley Kids #33, CAROLINE'S HALLOWEEN SPELL.

SWEET VALLEY KIDS

Jessica and Elizabeth have had lots of adventures in *Sweet Valley High* and *Sweet Valley Twins*...now read about the twins at age seven! You'll love all the fun that comes with being seven—birthday parties, playing dress-up, class projects, putting on puppet shows and plays, losing a tooth, setting up lemonade stands, caring for animals and much more! It's all part of SWEET VALLEY KIDS. Read them all!

☐ **JESSICA AND THE SPELLING BEE SURPRISE #21**　15917-8　$2.75

☐ **SWEET VALLEY SLUMBER PARTY #22**　15934-8　$2.75

☐ **LILA'S HAUNTED HOUSE PARTY # 23**　15919-4　$2.99

☐ **COUSIN KELLY'S FAMILY SECRET # 24**　15920-8　$2.75

☐ **LEFT-OUT ELIZABETH # 25**　15921-6　$2.99

☐ **JESSICA'S SNOBBY CLUB # 26**　15922-4　$2.99

☐ **THE SWEET VALLEY CLEANUP TEAM # 27**　15923-2　$2.99

☐ **ELIZABETH MEETS HER HERO #28**　15924-0　$2.99

☐ **ANDY AND THE ALIEN # 29**　15925-9　$2.99

☐ **JESSICA'S UNBURIED TREASURE # 30**　15926 7　$2.99

SWEET VALLEY TWINS.